FRESH CIDER and PIE

By FRANZ BRANDENBERG · Pictures by ALIKI

University Library **Macmillan Publishing Co., Inc./New York**
Collier Macmillan Publishers/London

The four-color illustrations were prepared as pen-and-ink line drawings, with halftone overlays for yellow, blue, and red. The typeface is Souvenir, with the title in Standle Wienerschnitzel.

Library of Congress Cataloging in Publication Data   Brandenberg, Franz. Fresh cider and pie.   [1. Stories in rhyme] I. Aliki, illus.
II. Title.   PZ8.3.B735Fr   73-585   ISBN 0-02-711910-6.

For Jason and Alexa
who drink all of their cider and leave none of their pie

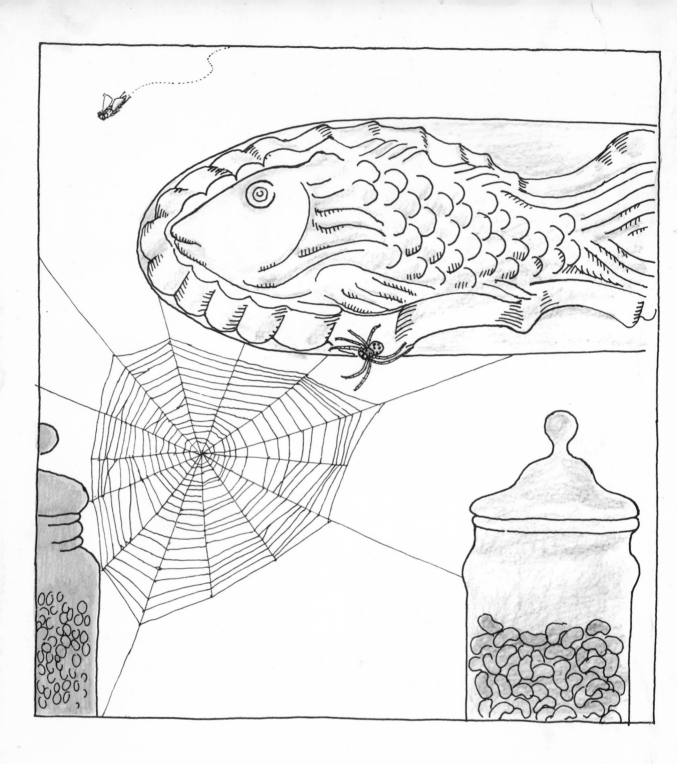

There was once a spider

who caught a fly.

"I am going to eat you," she said.
"Make your last wish."

"My favorite dish," said the fly,
"is apple pie with a glass of cider."
"Your wish shall be granted," said the spider.

The spider fetched the apples,

baked the pie,

and pressed the cider.

"Thank you very much, Miss Spider,"
said the fly,

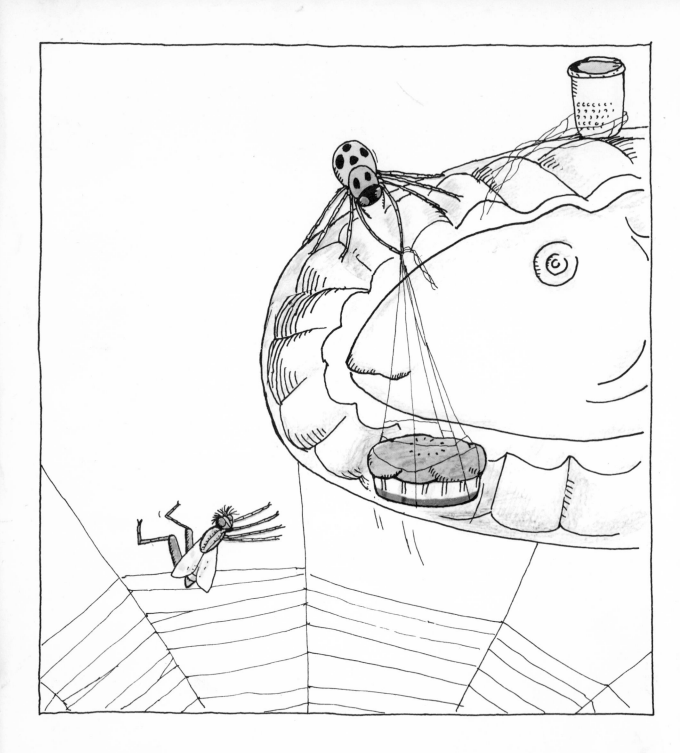

"for this good cider and pie."
"You are welcome," said the spider,

eating all of the pie
and leaving none of the cider.

"No fly has ever tasted such delicious pie,"
said the fly.

"Would you like a little more,
before you die?" asked the spider.
"I would indeed," said the fly.

The spider baked another pie.

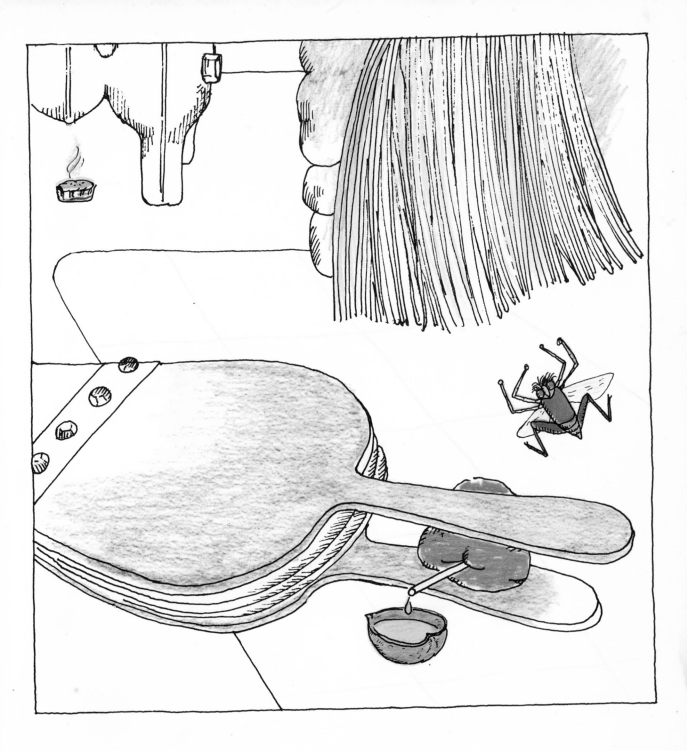

The fly pressed more cider.

Then the spider drank all of the cider

and left none of the pie.

"I didn't know," said the fly,
"that spiders are so good at making cider."

"Have some more!" said the spider.
"I won't say no," said the fly.

This time the spider pressed the cider

and the fly baked the pie.

For the third time the spider
guzzled down the cider

and the fly watched her eat the pie.

They carried on this way

for the rest of the day.

"I don't think there is any room in me,"
said the spider,

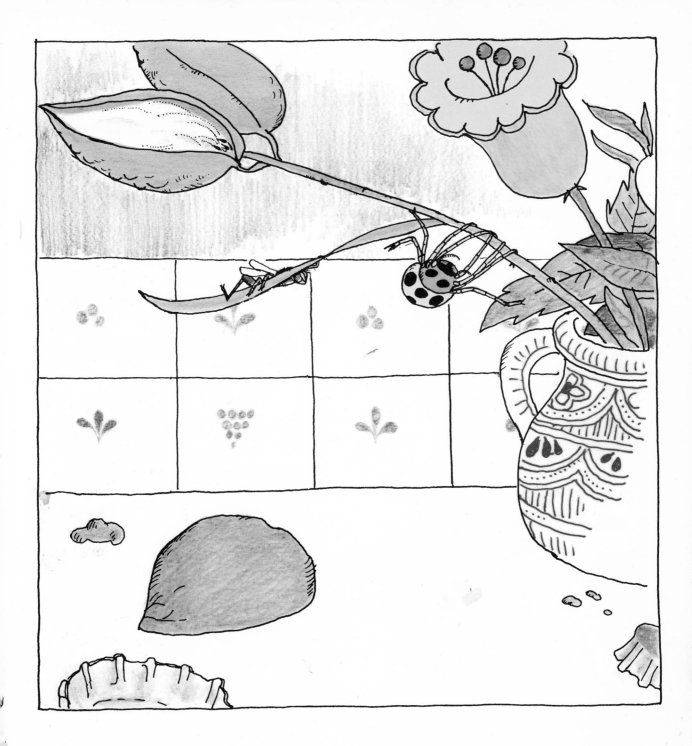

"for a fly full of pie and apple cider."

"It was a lovely day," said the fly.

"Good-by!"

THE END